THE DRAGON THANKSGIVING FEAST
THINGS TO MAKE AND DO

THE DRAGON THANKSGIVING FEAST

THINGS TO MAKE AND DO

WRITTEN AND ILLUSTRATED BY

LOREEN LEEDY

HOLIDAY HOUSE · NEW YORK

For DR. BRUCE

Printed in the United States of America
First Edition

Library of Congress Cataloging-in-Publication Data

Leedy, Loreen.
A dragon Thanksgiving feast : things to make and do / written and
illustrated by Loreen Leedy.—1st ed.
p.   cm.
Summary: Dragons celebrate Thanksgiving by preparing and enjoying
a great feast. Includes instructions for activities and games
related to the holiday.
ISBN 0-8234-0828-0
[1. Thanksgiving Day—Fiction.   2. Dragons—Fiction.   3. Stories
in rhyme.]   I. Title.
PZ8.3.L4995Du 1990
[E]—dc20   90-55110   CIP   AC
ISBN 0-8234-0828-0

The dragons howl at the harvest moon,
"Thanksgiving Day is coming soon!"

"Let's make a meal for everyone.
We'll cook and clean until we're done."

The dragons hike to gather weeds,
Leaves and vines and nuts and seeds.

They work to make some new creations,

WILD BIRD FEEDER

1. Find a large pinecone and tie string or wrap a pipe cleaner arou the end.

2. Spread pinecone with peanut b ter, then gently roll in wild bird see

3. Hang in a tree so birds can have Thanksgiving feast, too.

THANKS COLLAGE

1. Gather photographs, magazine clippings, and drawings of people, places, and things to be thankful for. Cut out letters WE ARE THANKFUL FOR from construction paper.

2. Arrange everything on a piece of poster board in a pleasing design. Glue or tape each item in place.

URKEY POPCORN HOLDER

. Cut the top off a brown bag, making it
en inches high. Glue 2-inch strips of
ardboard around top edge to stiffen.

. Cut a brown piece of construction
aper into 4 strips (lengthwise.) Cut a
inge into each strip, as shown.

. Starting along bottom edge of bag,
lue on rows of the fringed paper until
utside is covered.

. Cut out wings, head, eyes, bead,
attle, and tail from construction paper,
en glue in place. Let dry. Line turkey
ith a plastic bag, then fill with popcorn.

head

wing

eyes

beak

wattle

tail

EDIBLE NECKLACE

1. Gather small pretzels, and cereal and
candies with holes, as shown.

2. String on a 30-inch length of yarn. Tie
ends in a bow. Make a necklace for each
guest.

And simple table decorations.

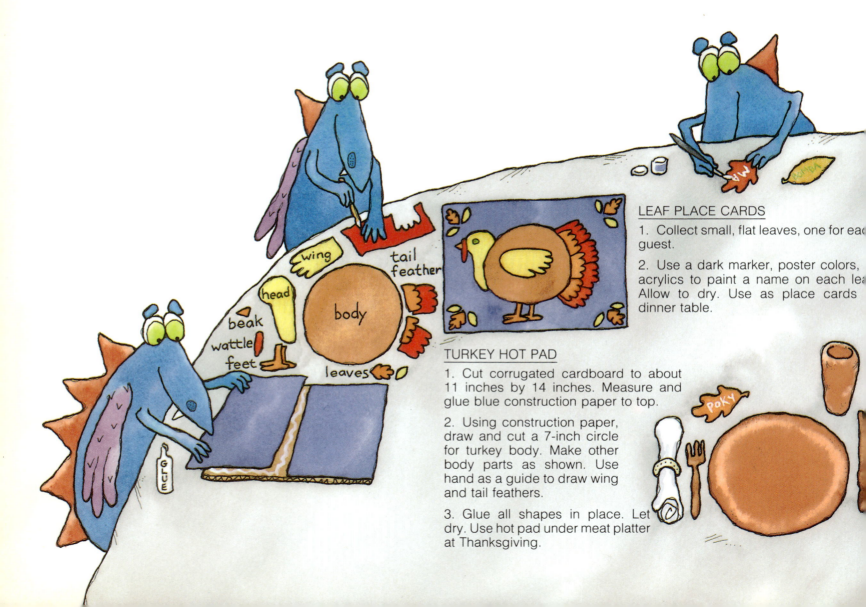

LEAF PLACE CARDS

1. Collect small, flat leaves, one for eac[h] guest.

2. Use a dark marker, poster colors, [or] acrylics to paint a name on each lea[f]. Allow to dry. Use as place cards [at] dinner table.

TURKEY HOT PAD

1. Cut corrugated cardboard to about 11 inches by 14 inches. Measure and glue blue construction paper to top.

2. Using construction paper, draw and cut a 7-inch circle for turkey body. Make other body parts as shown. Use hand as a guide to draw wing and tail feathers.

3. Glue all shapes in place. Let dry. Use hot pad under meat platter at Thanksgiving.

wing

head

beak

wattle

feet

body

tail feather

leaves

GLUE

POKY

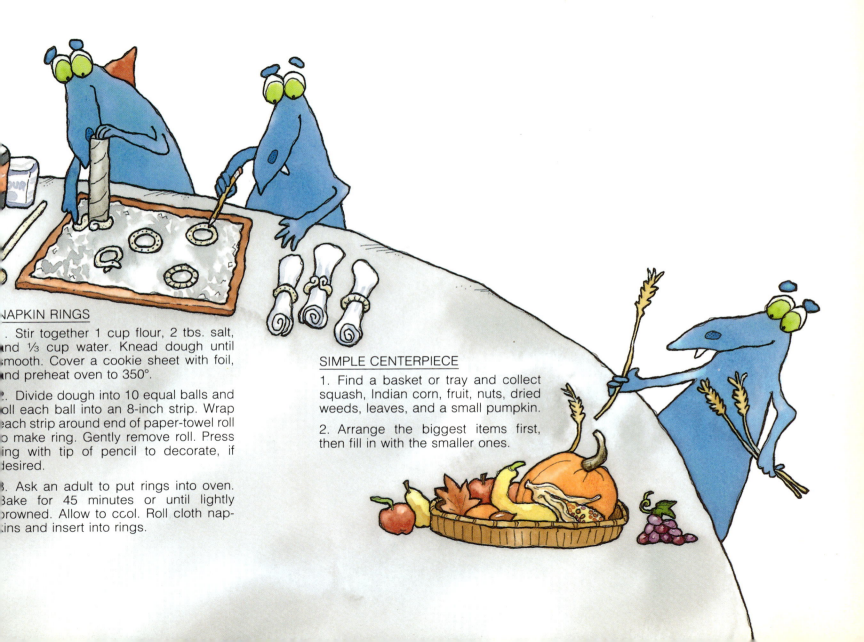

NAPKIN RINGS

1. Stir together 1 cup flour, 2 tbs. salt, and ⅓ cup water. Knead dough until smooth. Cover a cookie sheet with foil, and preheat oven to 350°.

2. Divide dough into 10 equal balls and roll each ball into an 8-inch strip. Wrap each strip around end of paper-towel roll to make ring. Gently remove roll. Press ring with tip of pencil to decorate, if desired.

3. Ask an adult to put rings into oven. Bake for 45 minutes or until lightly browned. Allow to cool. Roll cloth napkins and insert into rings.

SIMPLE CENTERPIECE

1. Find a basket or tray and collect squash, Indian corn, fruit, nuts, dried weeds, leaves, and a small pumpkin.

2. Arrange the biggest items first, then fill in with the smaller ones.

Then ten little dragons dig in the ground,
For crunchy vegetables by the pound.

They sift and measure, stir and heat,

PUMPKIN CORNBREAD

PREHEAT OVEN TO 425° F

SIFT
- 1½ C. cornmeal
- ½ C. whole-wheat flour
- 1 tbs. baking powder
- 3 tbs. sugar
- 1 tsp. cinnamon
- 1 tsp. salt

BEAT
- 1 egg
- 3 tbs. vegetable oil
- ¾ C. canned pumpkin
- 1½ C. milk

Stir quickly into dry ingredients, leaving a few lumps. Pour into an oiled 8"×8" pan. Bake 30-35 minutes. Cool for 10 minutes. Cut into squares.

PILGRIM PUNCH

Stir - 3 C. cranberry juice
         2 C. orange juice
         3 C. ginger ale

Add   - 3 scoops orange sherbet
Makes ½ gallon.

The food that dragons love to eat.

MAYFLOWER POTATO BOATS
PREHEAT OVEN TO 400°F
SCRUB — 1 large baking potato
for every 2 guests
Prick skin with fork several times.
Bake 1 hour, then cool enough to
handle. Cut each potato in half
lengthwise. Top each half
with butter, chives, salt, & pepper.

Have ready 1 slice American cheese
per potato half, and long toothpicks
(at least 3"). To make sail, carefully
poke toothpick through cheese slice.
Press sail into potato.
Serve boats immediately.

Their guests arrive from far away,
To celebrate the holiday.

A grand parade goes marching by,
Big balloons float in the sky.

The dragons play some games for fun,

And set the table for everyone.

WE ARE
THANKFUL
FOR

At last the feast is cooked and hot,
The dragons gobble it on the spot.

Then the dragons smile and say,
"What a great Thanksgiving Day!"

GOBBLE-AND-GIGGLE THANKSGIVING GAME

I Sailed on the Mayflower
(A memory game for two or more players.)

The first player begins by naming an object after saying the refrain, "I sailed on the Mayflower and what did I take?" For example: "I sailed on the Mayflower and what did I take? I took a *tall Pilgrim hat.*"

The next player repeats the refrain and the first object, then mentions a new object. For example: "I sailed on the Mayflower and what did I take? I took a tall Pilgrim hat and a *fat piglet.*"

Each player must remember all the previous items and add another to the list. If a player can't remember, he or she is OUT. The player with the best memory is the winner.

Pin-the-Tail-on-the-Turkey

Draw a turkey on a big piece of paper or poster board, but don't give him a tail. Fasten securely on the wall, or on the back of a large piece of furniture.

Draw feathers on construction paper and cut them out. Add a piece of tape to each feather. Blindfold players and write their names on the feathers. Turn players around once, then direct them toward the turkey. The players try to place the feathers where the turkey's tail is missing. The player who places the feather closest to where the tail should be is the winner.

Count the Popcorn

Fill a large glass jar with popcorn kernels. Each player examines the jar and tries to guess the number of kernels. Then the player writes down his guess and name on a piece of paper. When the players have finished, everyone counts the kernels. Whoever came closest to the actual number is the winner. When the game is over, ask an adult to pop the popcorn. Then everyone can gobble it up!

My two Book

by Jane Belk Moncure
illustrated by Pam Peltier

THE CHILD'S WORLD
MANKATO, MN 56001

Library of Congress Cataloging in Publication Data

Moncure, Jane Belk.
  My two book.

  Summary: Little Two introduces the concept
of "two" by interacting with two of a variety of things.
    1. Two (The number)—Juvenile literature.
[1. Two (the number)   2. Number concept.   3. Counting]
I. Peltier, Pam, ill.   II. Title.
QA141.3.M664 1985   513'.2   85-7885
ISBN 0-89565-313-3 -1991 Edition

My  Book

This is Little

Little  lives in . . .

the house
of two.

It has two rooms.
Count them. One. Two.

5

The house of two has two front doors . . .
and two front windows.

Count them.

Everyday Little  puts on her . . .

two shoes

and goes for a walk.

One day she found
two caterpillars.

After that, everyday she stopped to see them.

Little by little the caterpillars changed.

Everyday she
watched and waited. Guess what?

One day out flew two butterflies.

One.

Two.

Little clapped two claps. Can you?

Little  caught one of the butterflies, but . . .

it was sad, so . . .

11

she let it go.

How many butterflies flew away?

Little  hopped two hops and found . . .

two hens.

The hens said,
"Cluck, cluck"
two times. Can you?

13

Then the hens flew away.

Little saw two eggs.

Guess what?

The eggs cracked open.

Out hopped two little chicks.
The chicks said, "Peep, peep"
two times. Can you?

15

Little  caught one chick, but . . .

the chick was sad.

So Little  let it go.

How many baby chicks went hop, hop?

Later Little  found two lambs.

The lambs were sad. "We are lost," they said.

"We want our mamas!"

Little  said, "Let's find them.
"Come along."

19

Little  found one . . .

mama
sheep.

How many mamas were still missing?

20

Little  found the other mama sheep.

How many are in the pen?

Next Little  found . . .

two tadpoles.

She put the two tadpoles in a . . .

bowl.

She waited two weeks. Guess what?

The tadpoles grew into frogs.
How many?

Little  said, "Hop, hop."

The two frogs went hop, hop. Can you?

25

Then Little  saw . . .

two stars in the sky.

"I must go home," she said .

26

She yawned two yawns. Can you?

She took off two shoes. One, two.
Then she found . . .

two teddy bears

and two blankets.

Little  hopped, "hop, hop," into bed.

And she went to sleep in two winks.

Extra Pages

Little  found two of everything.

two lambs

two caterpillars

two sheep

two butterflies

two tadpoles

two hens

two frogs

two eggs

two teddy bears

two chicks

two stars

Now you find two things

ittle 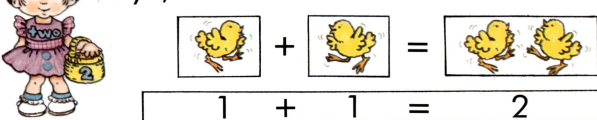 says, "Let's add."

1	+	1	=	2

2	+	0	=	2

'Let's take away."

2	–	1	=	1

2	–	2	=	0

31

Extra
Pages

"See what I made," said Little 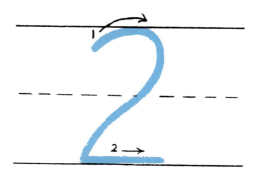.
She makes a 2 this way:

Then she makes the word "two"
like this: _____

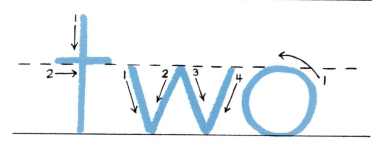

You can make them in the air with your fingers.